To the totally awesome Ms ["A...]
Our future leaders a
hands.
Louie Lawene

LOUIE LAWENT

ZOEY THE PIG

Illustrated by Phoebe Cho

Created by Louie Lawent and Tim Helstad

Histria Kids
Las Vegas • Chicago • Palm Beach

Published in the United States of America by
Histria Books, a division of Histria LLC
7181 N. Hualapai Way, Ste. 130-86
Las Vegas, NV 89166 USA
HistriaBooks.com

Histria Kids is an imprint of Histria Books. Titles published under the imprints of Histria Books are distributed worldwide.

All rights reserved. No part of this book may be reprinted or reproduced or utilized in any form or by any electronic, mechanical or other means, now known or hereafter invented, including photocopying and recording, or in any information storage or retrieval system, without the permission in writing from the Publisher.

Library of Congress Control Number: 2022938666
ISBN 978-1-59211-184-8 (casebound)
ISBN 978-1-59211-220-3 (eBook)

Copyright © 2022 by Louie Lawent

Zoey the Pig was the fattest pig in the county, eight hundred pounds of corn plopped into one big pile of pig. Zoey, also known as Old Grandma Zoey, lived alone in a small shed on the back acre of Farmer Gruder's farm in Bouchie Gouchie Town.

At least Farmer Gruder called it Bouchie Gouchie Town. Other townsfolk called it Bumper Rumper Ville.

This silly quarrel had gone on for as long as anybody could remember. Zoey called the town Bumper Rumper Ville just to irritate Farmer Gruder, even though she really believed the correct name was Bouchie Gouchie Town.

Now if you thought that Old Grandma Zoey had a big belly, would you ever be in shock when she turned around on her creaky old knees and modeled that backside.

And if she spun around too fast ... boom ... rumbum ... crash! No, that's not an earthquake. That's Zoey losing her balance.

Poor Zoey. That's not the only thing she lost. She lost her lunch pail and her hairbrush. She even lost track of the lies she told. But she never lost what she needed to lose most, two hundred pounds of her backside. You know how it is when your mom and dad tell you to do something you don't want to do and you make excuses? You say, "I would have picked up my toys but …" "I would have studied harder but …" Or "I would have been nicer to my friend but …" Well, if you added up all the "buts" you ever used in your life, you still wouldn't have as big a problem as Zoey.

But at least some creatures found it useful.

For instance, when Zoey fell asleep in a mudhole, all the other pigs would draw a map of the world on Zoey and stand where they drew the Atlantic Ocean.

Then they would spring up from this homemade Zoey diving board, soar into the air, and plunge headfirst into the mud. My what fun!

Now Zoey and a few of the other pigs in town were different from the rest of the pigs, for Zoey and her chums could walk like human beings. Zoey considered herself special and verbally rubbed the faces of the ordinary pigs into the dirt because of it. And though she was called "Old Grandma Zoey," she had a baby face and acted like one. And you didn't dare criticize her. If you did, she would always give the same response. Like when Farmer Gruder said, "Hurry up and mow the grass, Zoey!" Zoey would stomp on the ground and holler, "I'LL GIVE YOU AN EGG!"

Or how about when Herbie the Horse politely said, "I know you're busy, Zoey, but you didn't pour me enough water." Zoey yelled back, "Water you say! Well, I say, 'I'LL GIVE YOU AN EGG.'" But everybody loved Zoey anyway because she told the wildest stories and tickled herself until she tumbled down from exhaustion.

Well, Farmer Gruder owned Zoey and assigned her daily chores to do, like feeding corn to the other pigs in their pens and cleaning the horses' stables. Since Zoey could walk, he also took her to county fairs.

He played the electric guitar, while Zoey danced, juggled bicycle tires, and tweeted like a songbird, all at the same time.

One day, a very angry Zoey told Farmer Gruder, "I work my eight hundred pounds of fat off for you for practically nothing. I want more money. I want an easier job, like taste-testing your crops, like the lettuce, corn, and potatoes, to make sure they're of the highest quality."

Farmer Gruder responded, "I wouldn't let you taste-test an old pair of socks for holes in the toes. The last time you tasted my corn, you couldn't control your appetite and

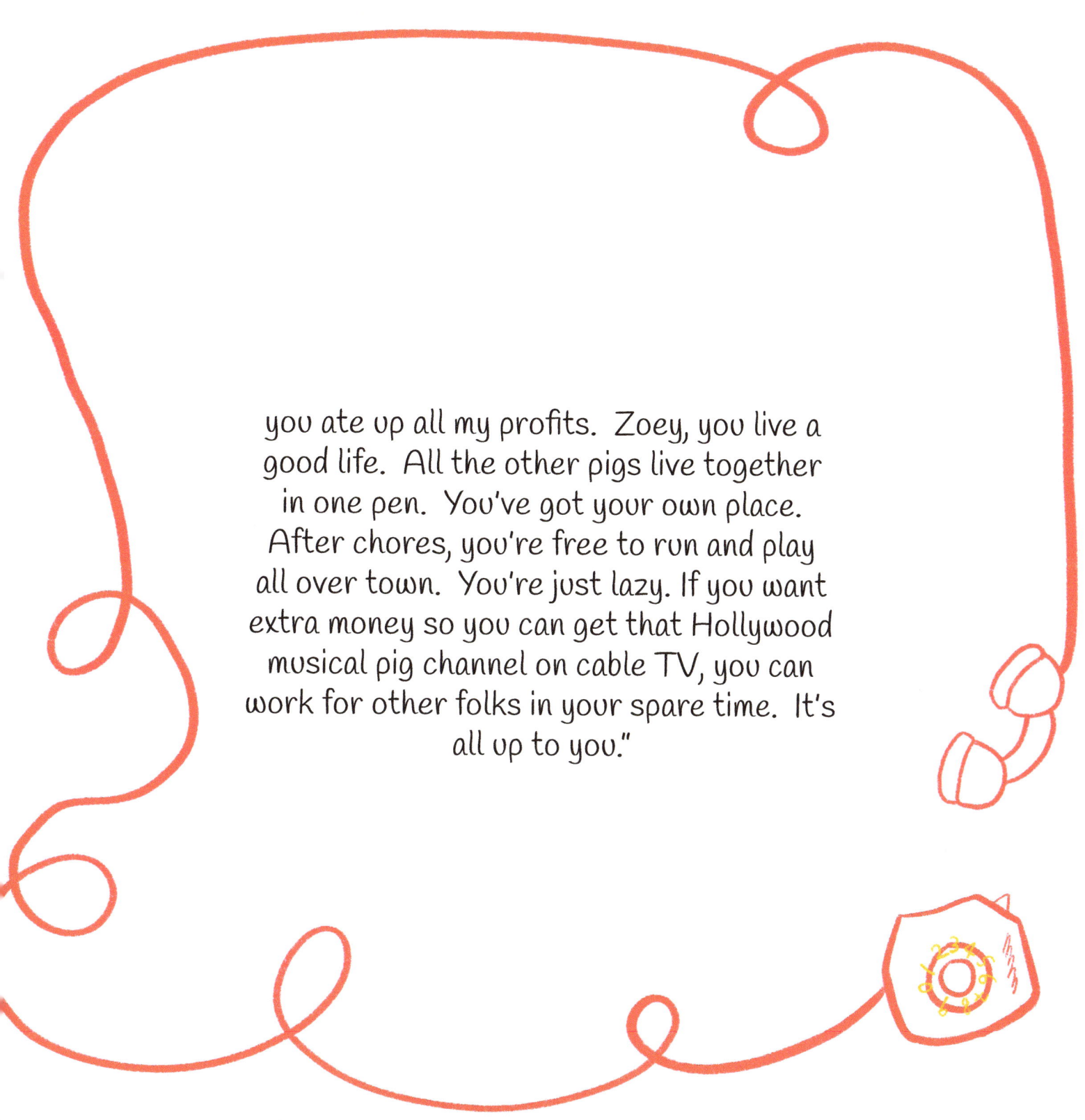

you ate up all my profits. Zoey, you live a good life. All the other pigs live together in one pen. You've got your own place. After chores, you're free to run and play all over town. You're just lazy. If you want extra money so you can get that Hollywood musical pig channel on cable TV, you can work for other folks in your spare time. It's all up to you."

Farmer Gruder strolled away, while Old Grandma Zoey got so red-hot mad she thought she was going to blow up. Finally, she shook her fist and yelled, "I'LL GIVE YOU AN EGG!"

Well, Zoey had to think of something. She had big pig dreams. She wanted a larger shed with a gigantic indoor mudhole. She wanted brightly colored balloons shaped like Monopoly games hanging on her walls. She wanted to hire a talking goose to cook her meals and feed her peanuts and candy while she slopped around in the messy, slushy mudhole and watched cable TV.

But Zoey couldn't figure out what to do, so she called a club meeting of her cohorts in slime. Over to her shed they came.

It was a tight squeeze, but the pigs gathered around her table. There was Hoover, dressed in her gas-station suit with a gas pump on her back; Clunky, with his usual bumps from his usual falls; and Gloober, with eyes on the far sides of his head.

Well, Zoey explained her problem. She wanted to make money and make it as easily as possible. Hoover suggested, "Why don't you paint the other animals' toenails when they want to look nice for Friday fish-fry parties?"

Zoey replied, "Too hard. My hands will be so tired, I won't be able to lie down and use my remote control to change TV channels."

Clunky suggested, "Why don't you teach the youngsters how to play soccer?"

"No way," Zoey said. "My legs will be too tired to make trips to the refrigerator when I get home."

Gloober suggested, "Why don't you help the goats crush soda pop cans with your teeth at the recycling center?"

Zoey scoffed, "You've got to be kidding! I don't use my mouth for anything I can't personally eat."

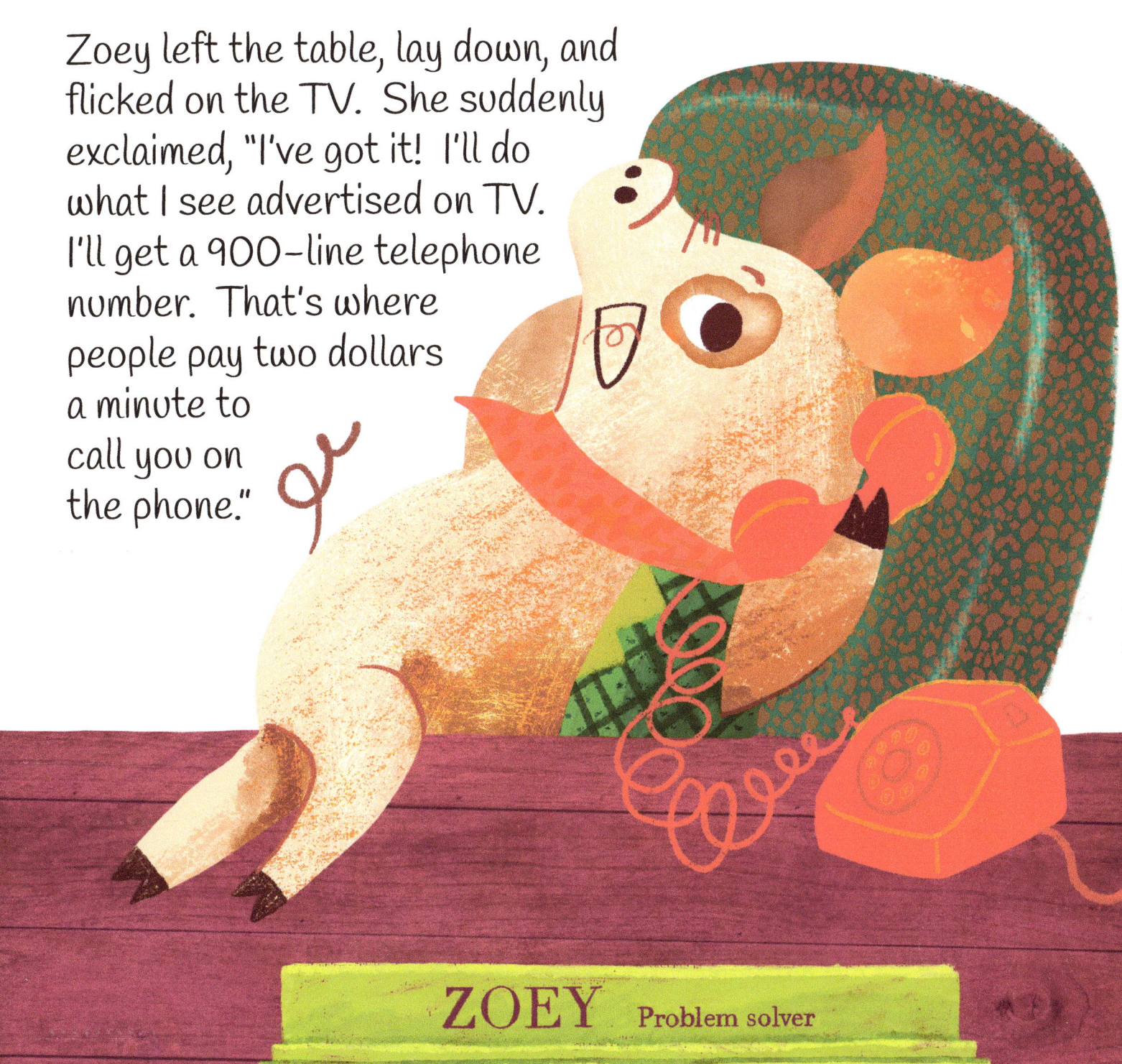

Zoey left the table, lay down, and flicked on the TV. She suddenly exclaimed, "I've got it! I'll do what I see advertised on TV. I'll get a 900-line telephone number. That's where people pay two dollars a minute to call you on the phone."

ZOEY   Problem solver

Gloober's eyes rolled to the middle of his head as he said, "Why would someone pay two dollars a minute to talk to you?"

Zoey answered, "Because I'll be 'Zoey the Problem Solver.' I'll give advice to solve people's problems."

Hoover laughed, then said, "You can't even solve your own problems."

Clunky looked very concerned. He said, "You're not qualified to do that, Zoey. That's a professional's job, not yours!"

Zoey shook her head. "Well, I'm doing it. I'll get rich and I can lie down while I work."

In disgust, Clunky, Gloober, and Hoover walked away. Hoover said, "You're lazy, Grandma Zoey. We gave you three good ideas. You're going to hurt someone with bad advice. Goodbye."

Zoey stormed to the door and shouted, "I'LL GIVE YOU AN EGG!"

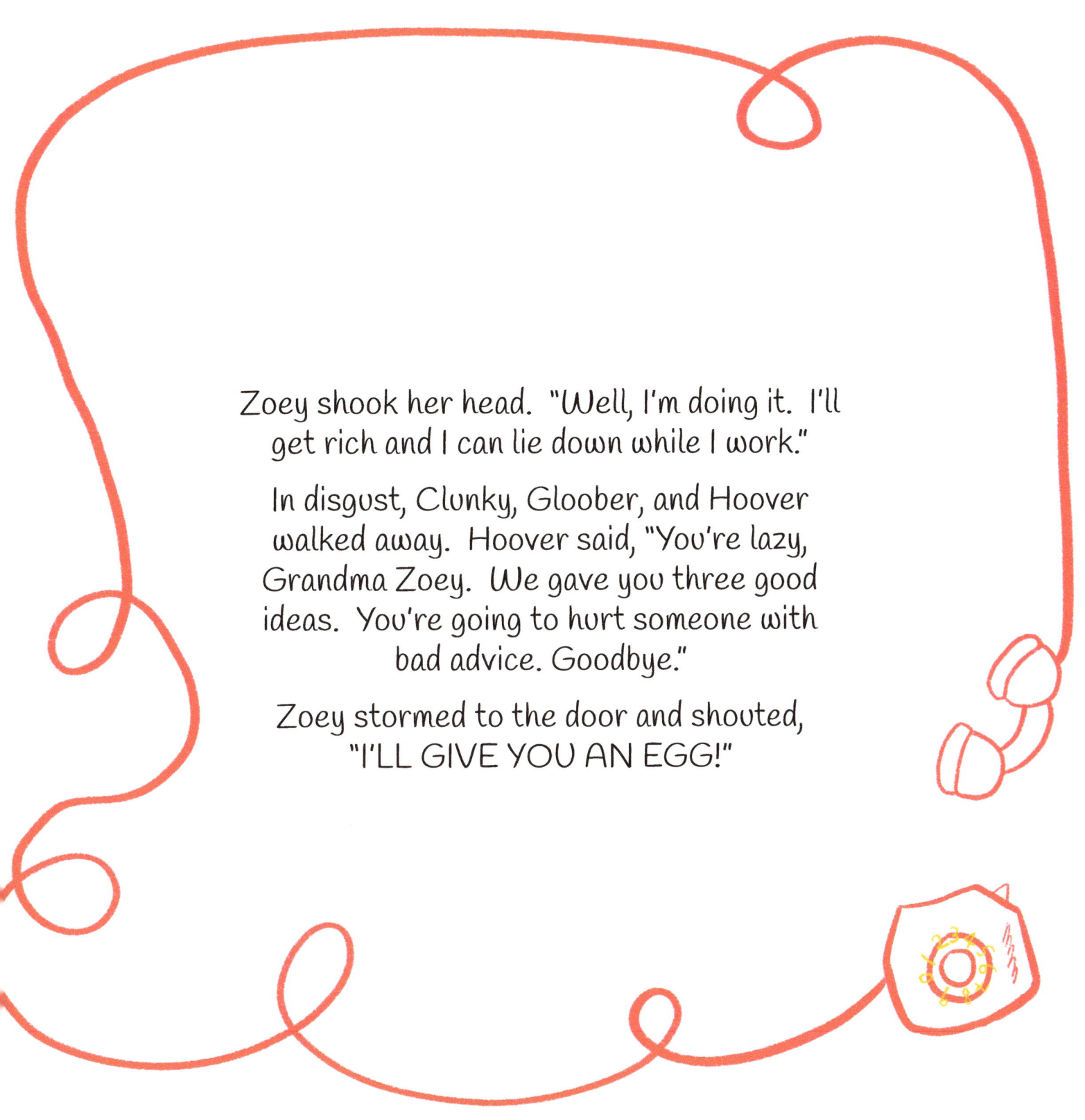

Well, Zoey set up her 900-line telephone number and handed out paper advertisements to all of the kids in town.

Zoey thought the adults would be jealous of her idea and tell their children not to call her, so she made the kids promise not to tell anyone about it.

Every night the calls came streaming in. Here are just a few.

Zoey answered, "Zoey's Problem Line. Who's calling?"

"Hi, Zoey, this is Billy. I have allergies and have to blow my nose a lot. My mom makes me take medicine, but I hate taking it. What should I do? I'd rather blow my nose than take the medicine."

Zoey unthinkingly replied, "Never do what you don't want to do. Be glad you have a nose to blow. I say, use it or lose it. Show your parents you mean business. Blow it at the dinner table. Blow it loud, blow it proud, blow it like you are the leader of the band. You've got melody son. Blow 'When the Saints Come Marching In'

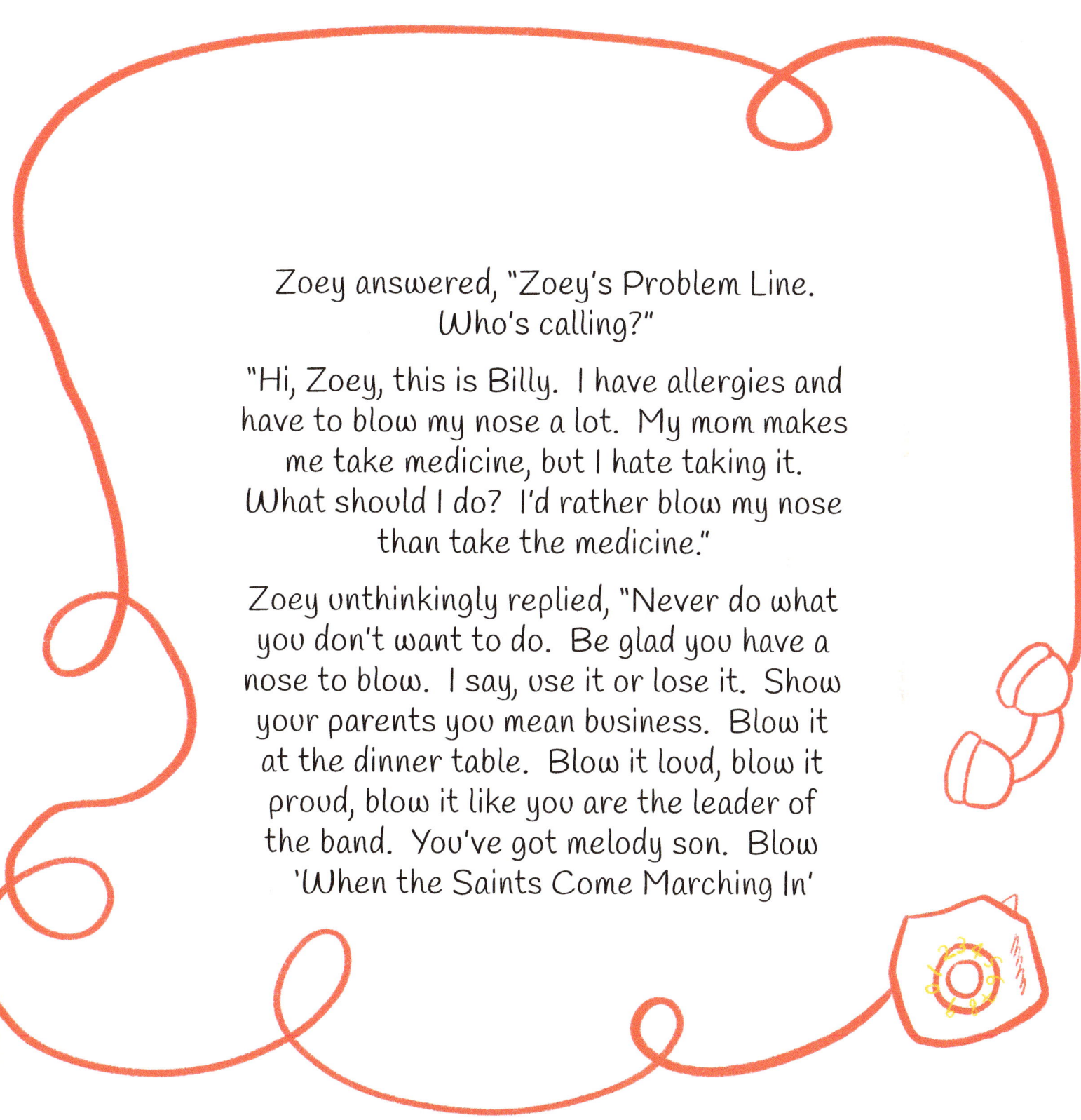

while you eat your peas. Then throw your handkerchief in with the dirty dishes. Let your mom worry about it. Billy, I bet you scrunch up your face because the medicine tastes bad and then your parents think you look cute, shoot a video of this nonsense, and sell it to some silly TV show where the joke's on you, Billy boy. Your parents make big money off of your pain and spend it on grown-up toys. Nuts to that!"

Billy happily coughed. "Thank you, Grandma Zoey. I can't wait for dinner. I'm going to practice my nose blows right now."

"Ring, Ring, Ring." Zoey picked up the phone.

"Hi, Zoey. I'm Toby, and I'm seven years old and still wet my bed. My parents are trying to get me in the habit of going to the bathroom, so they wake me up in the middle of the night while I'm sound asleep. I'm sick of it!"

Zoey said, "That's cruel. Why should you be inconvenienced? There are parents in Oregon who would love to have a kid like you. Bedwetters are a prized possession. They have contests and everything. Matter of fact, if their children don't wet the bed, they get rid of them, sell 'em to the garbagemen.

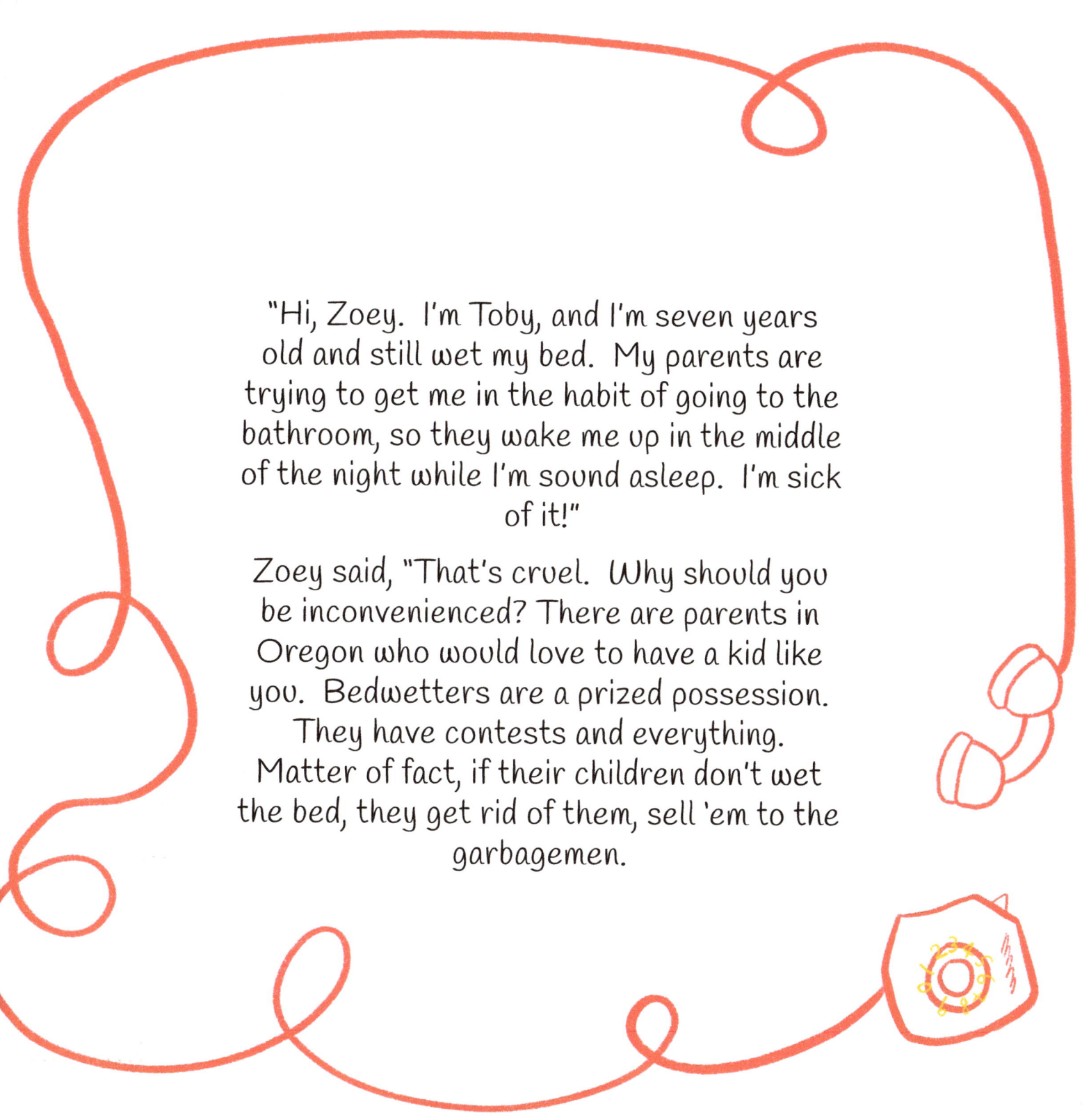

The parents say that the bedwetters are a good-luck charm. They're so proud of their liquid lads' accomplishments that they hang up the bedsheets in museums and call them pieces of art.

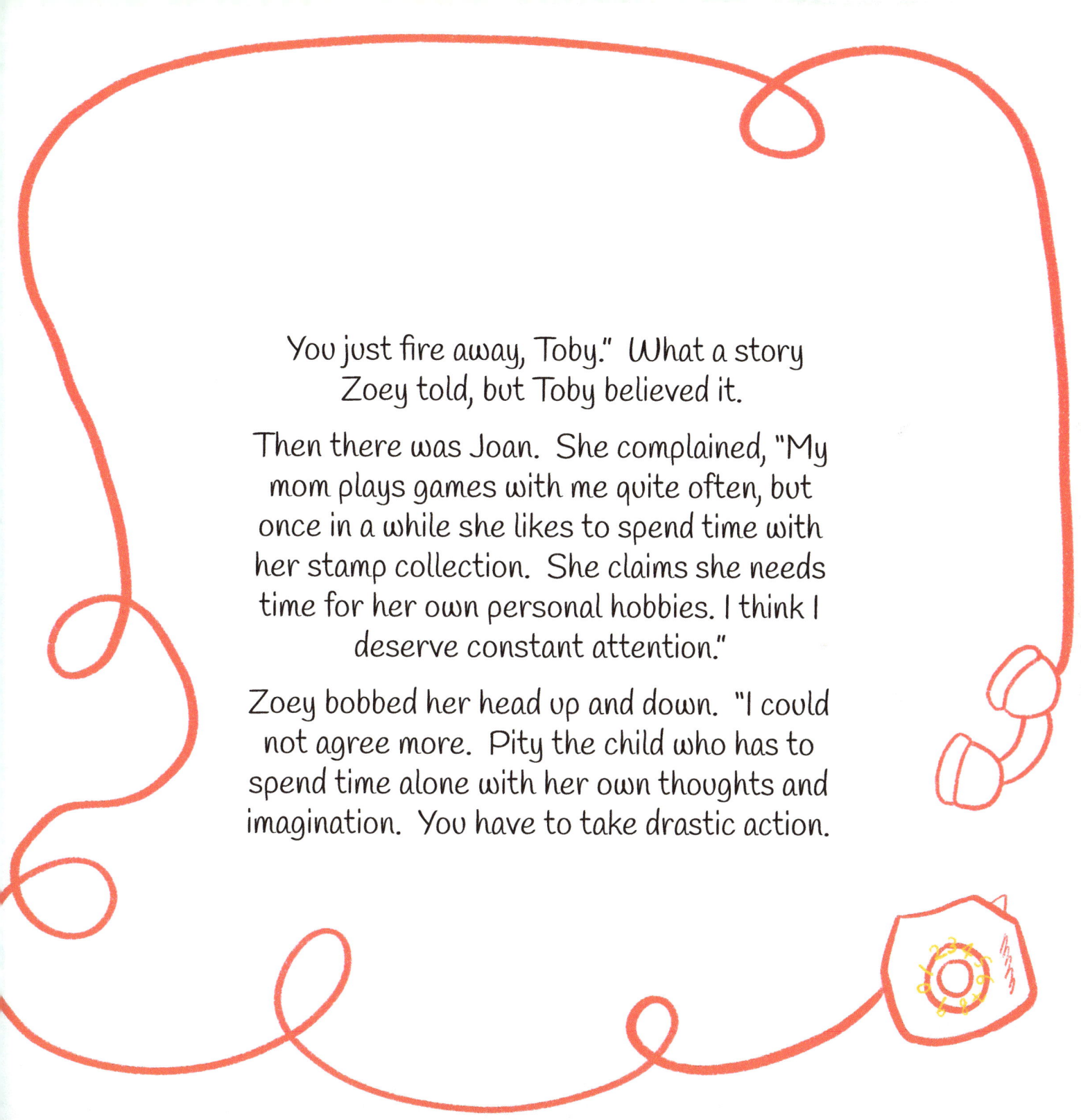

You just fire away, Toby." What a story Zoey told, but Toby believed it.

Then there was Joan. She complained, "My mom plays games with me quite often, but once in a while she likes to spend time with her stamp collection. She claims she needs time for her own personal hobbies. I think I deserve constant attention."

Zoey bobbed her head up and down. "I could not agree more. Pity the child who has to spend time alone with her own thoughts and imagination. You have to take drastic action.

Take all those stamps and stick them on a hooting owl. Tell your mom that you had to send a special delivery. As the bird flies away with the stamps, shout, 'Owl be seeing you.' Get it?"

And the calls continued to pour in day after day. Grandma Zoey could hear the cash register ringing in her head. But there was big trouble in Bouchie Gouchie Town. Or should I say Bumper Rumper Ville?

Some children wouldn't take their medicine and got sick. Some kids wouldn't take "no" for an anwer. Others acted rudely, talking back to their parents and neighbors.

All of the children who called Zoey cried every time they didn't get their way. No adult knew why.

Finally, one day Zoey got a call from Sally. Zoey answered the phone but noticed she was running late for her weekly card game with her dreaded rival, Old Grandma Skunk. Sally began, "My mom makes me do homework..."

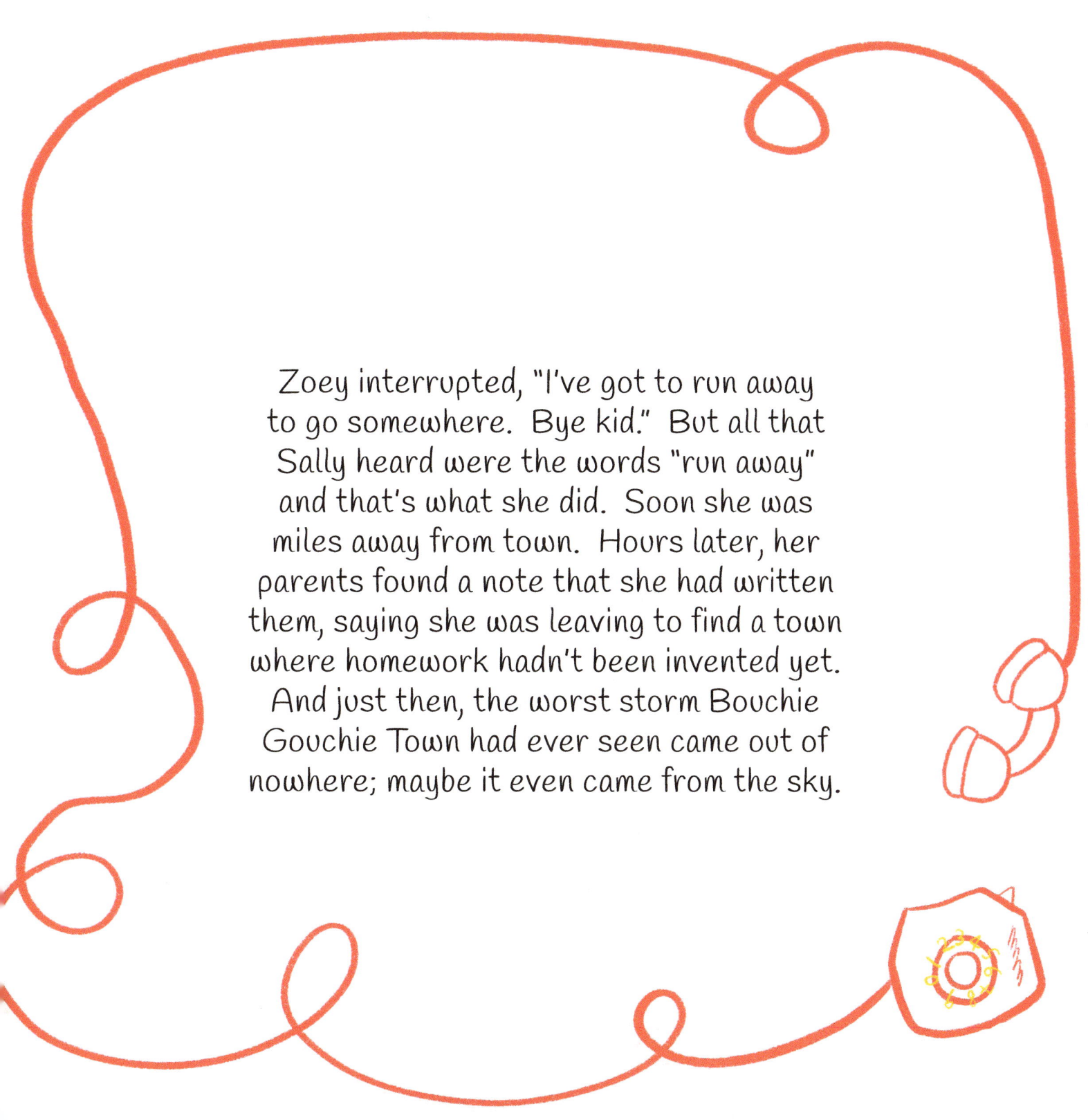

Zoey interrupted, "I've got to run away to go somewhere. Bye kid." But all that Sally heard were the words "run away" and that's what she did. Soon she was miles away from town. Hours later, her parents found a note that she had written them, saying she was leaving to find a town where homework hadn't been invented yet. And just then, the worst storm Bouchie Gouchie Town had ever seen came out of nowhere; maybe it even came from the sky.

The sky turned the deepest black in history. The thunder was louder than a Grandma Zoey burp and it rained so hard that the river flooded and washed out all of the roads leading out of town.

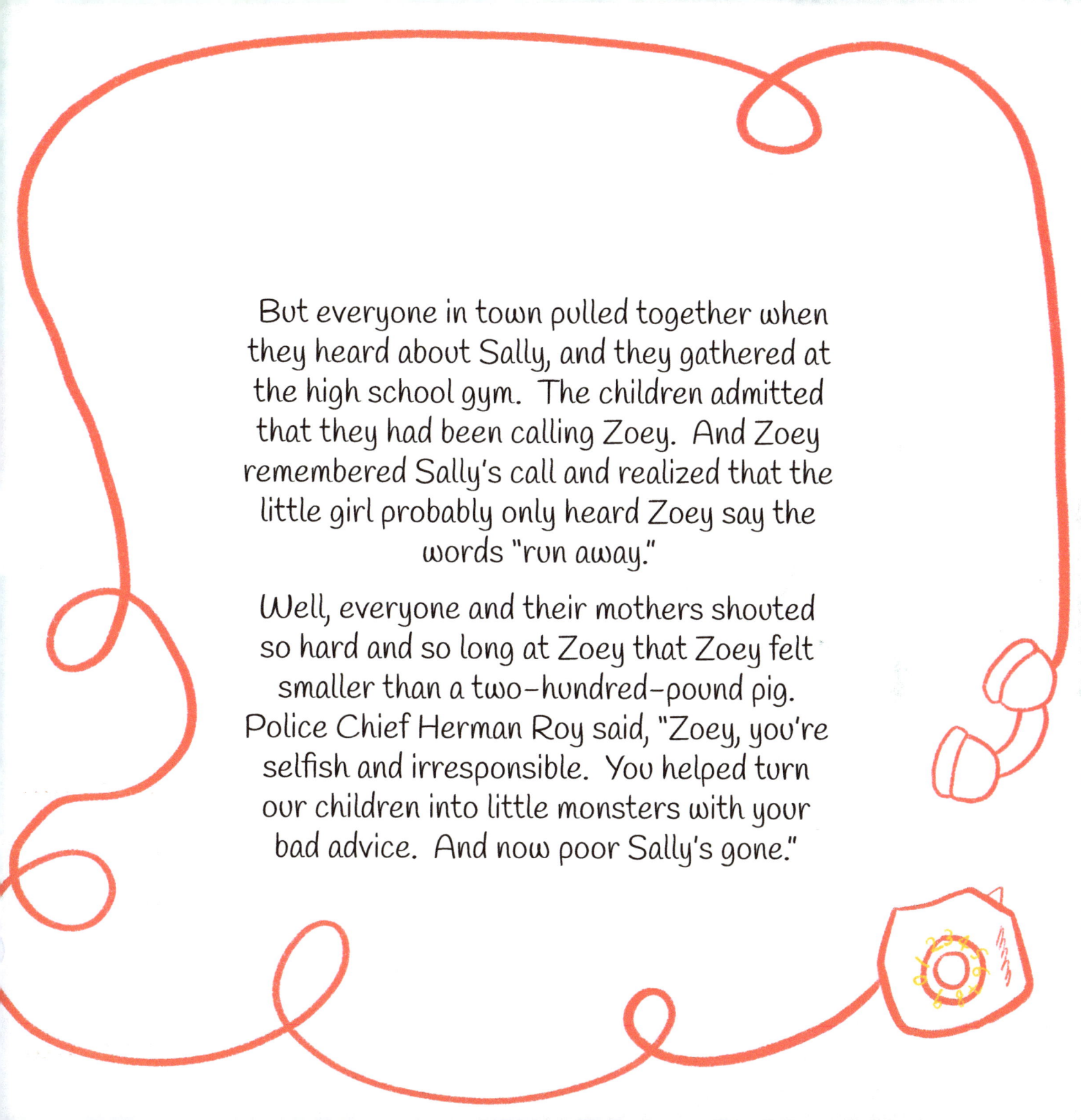

But everyone in town pulled together when they heard about Sally, and they gathered at the high school gym. The children admitted that they had been calling Zoey. And Zoey remembered Sally's call and realized that the little girl probably only heard Zoey say the words "run away."

Well, everyone and their mothers shouted so hard and so long at Zoey that Zoey felt smaller than a two-hundred-pound pig. Police Chief Herman Roy said, "Zoey, you're selfish and irresponsible. You helped turn our children into little monsters with your bad advice. And now poor Sally's gone."

Zoey couldn't stand it anymore and started to say, "I'll give you an..." but Zoey knew that this time she was in the wrong – all the way.

Farmer Gruder hung his head and said, "This is Bouchie Gouchie Town's saddest hour," which only started a big argument.

Half of the people shouted, "This is Bumper Rumper Ville!" The other half shouted, "This is Bouchie Gouchie Town!" And on and on it went. "Bumper Rumper Ville!" "No, it's Bouchie Gouchie Town!" "Bumper Rumper Ville!" "Bouchie Gouchie Town."

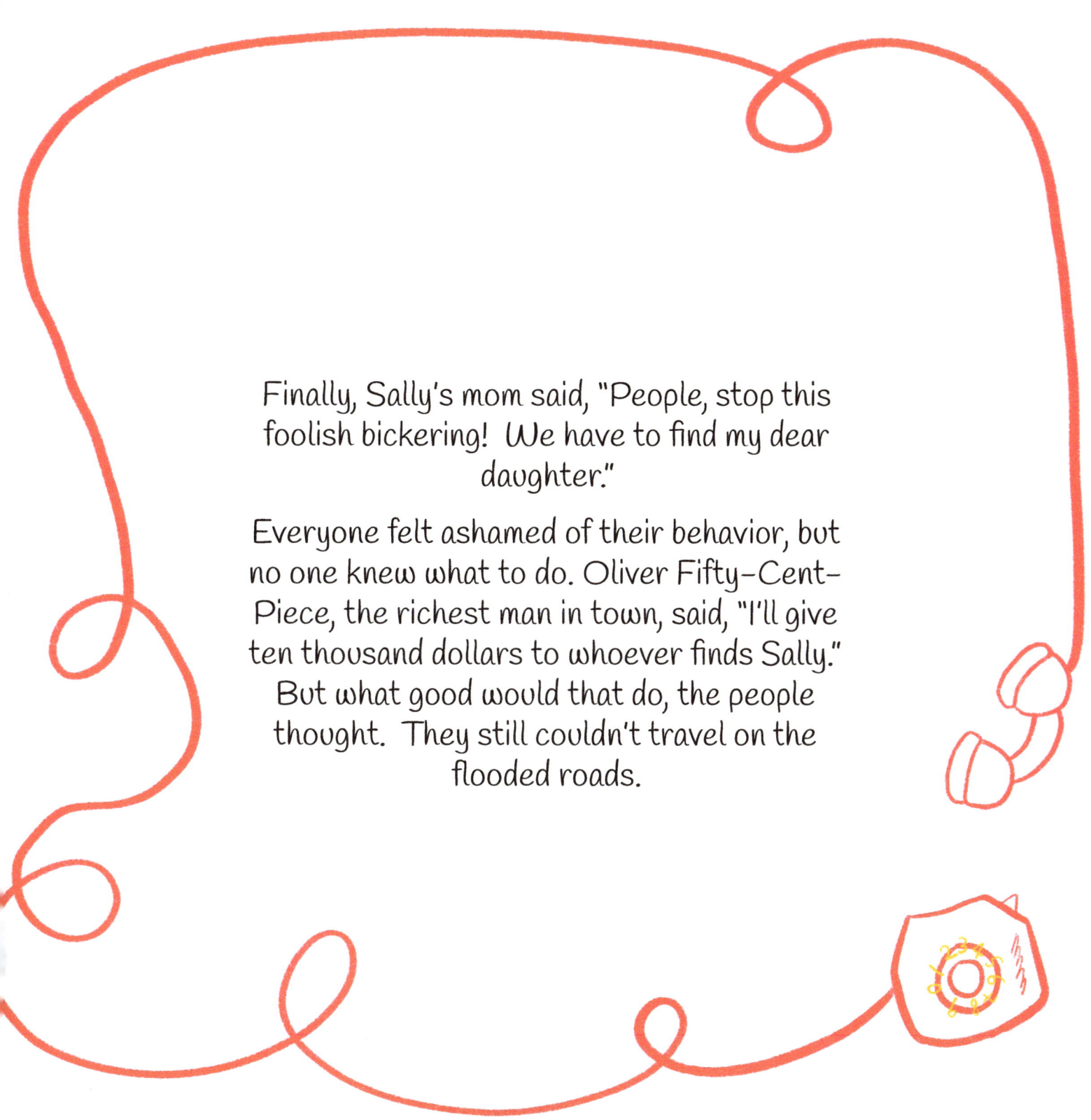

Finally, Sally's mom said, "People, stop this foolish bickering! We have to find my dear daughter."

Everyone felt ashamed of their behavior, but no one knew what to do. Oliver Fifty-Cent-Piece, the richest man in town, said, "I'll give ten thousand dollars to whoever finds Sally." But what good would that do, the people thought. They still couldn't travel on the flooded roads.

Old Grandma Skunk and her gang of wicked skunks suddenly got an idea. And so did Zoey and her group of friends. Grandma Skunk and Grandma Zoey each owned hot-air balloons.

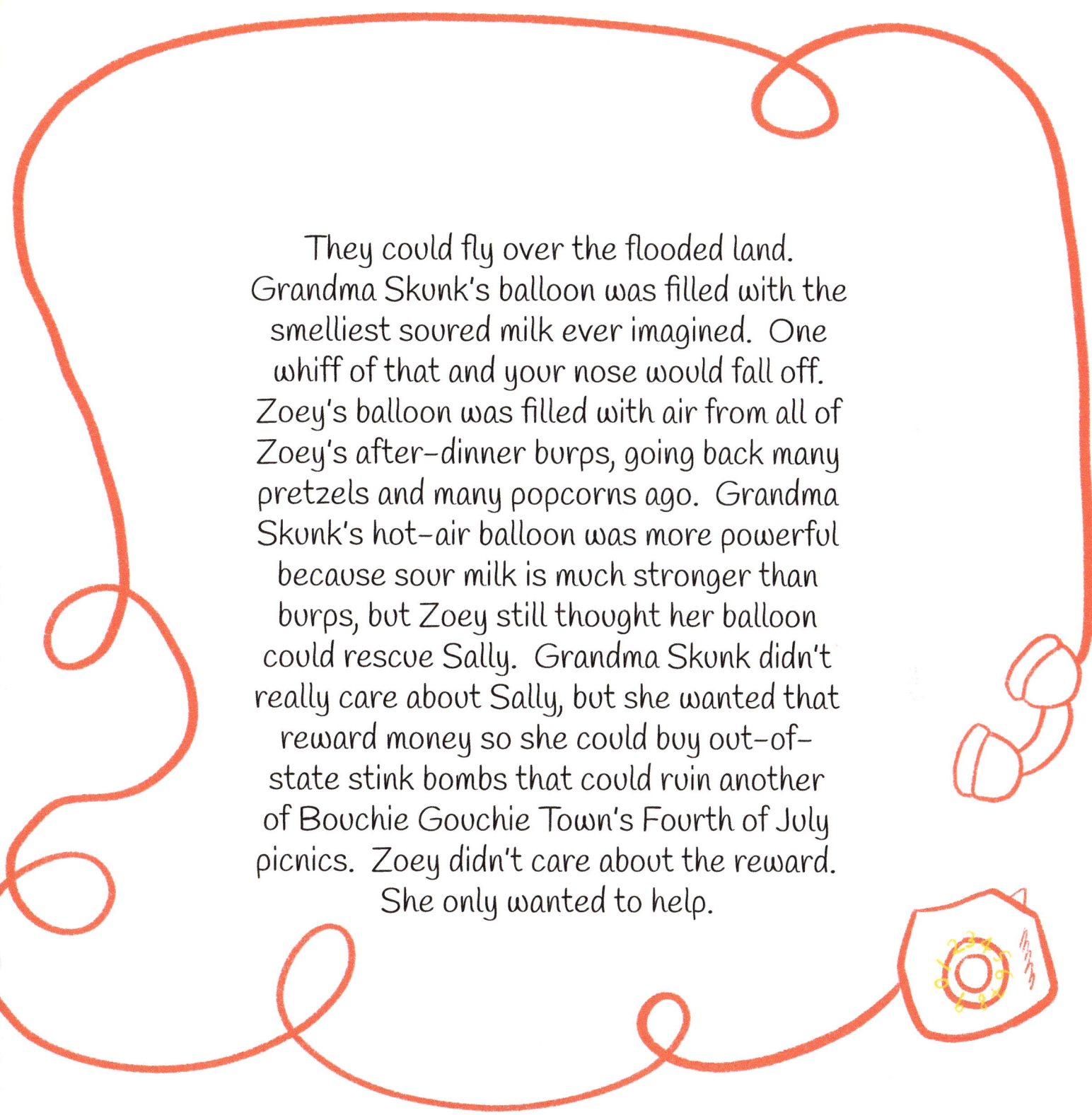

They could fly over the flooded land. Grandma Skunk's balloon was filled with the smelliest soured milk ever imagined. One whiff of that and your nose would fall off. Zoey's balloon was filled with air from all of Zoey's after-dinner burps, going back many pretzels and many popcorns ago. Grandma Skunk's hot-air balloon was more powerful because sour milk is much stronger than burps, but Zoey still thought her balloon could rescue Sally. Grandma Skunk didn't really care about Sally, but she wanted that reward money so she could buy out-of-state stink bombs that could ruin another of Bouchie Gouchie Town's Fourth of July picnics. Zoey didn't care about the reward. She only wanted to help.

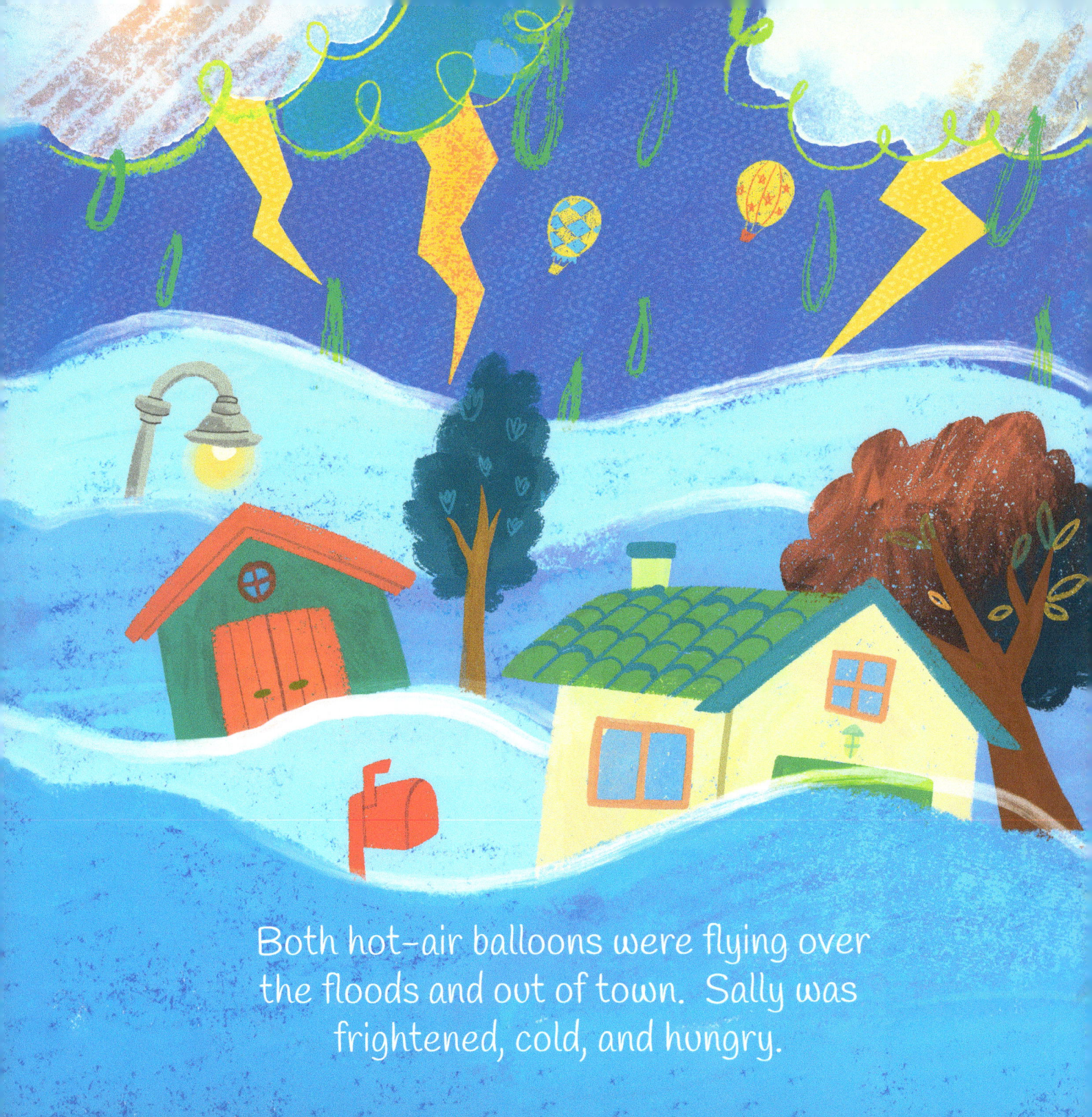

Both hot-air balloons were flying over the floods and out of town. Sally was frightened, cold, and hungry.

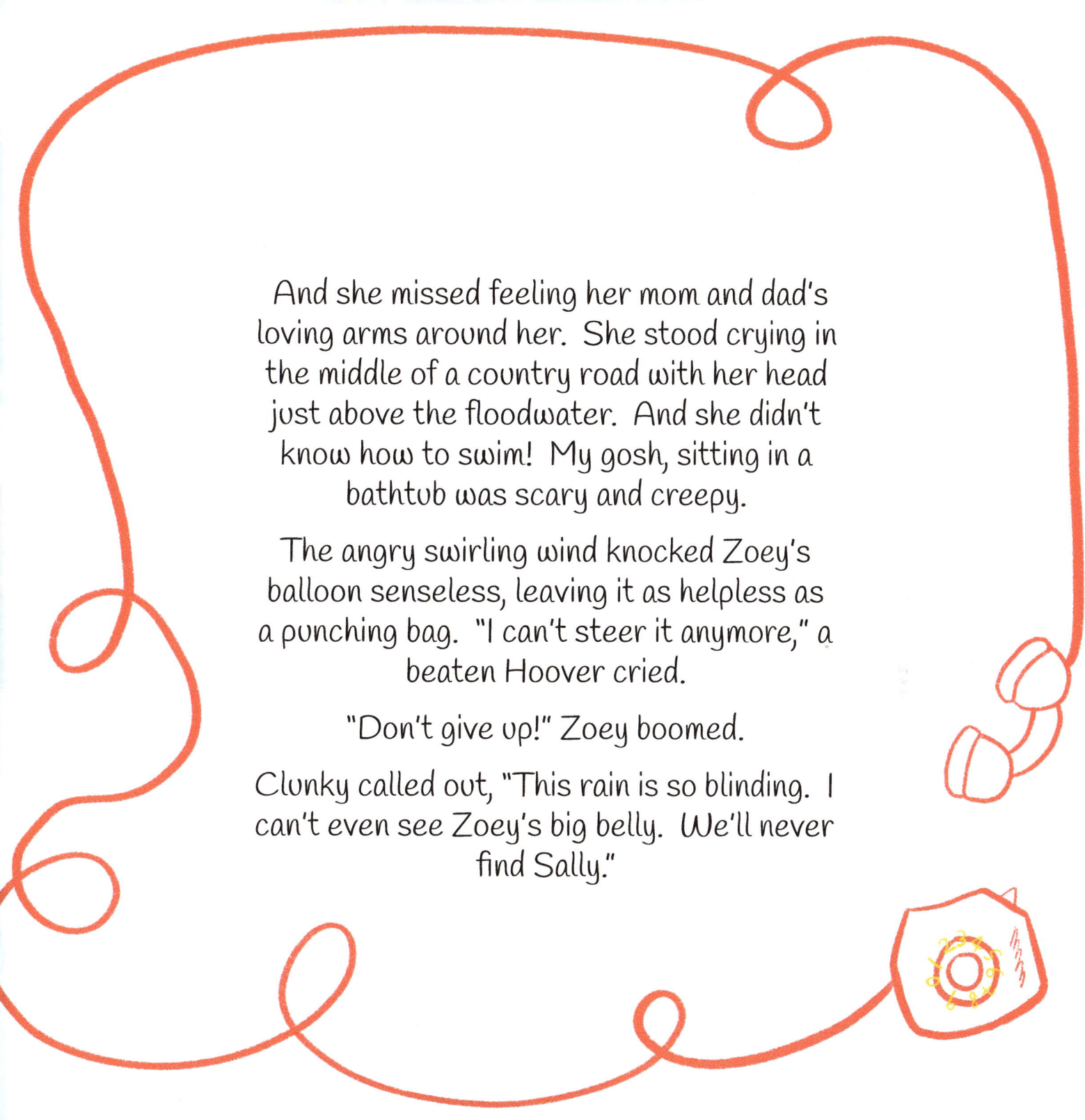

And she missed feeling her mom and dad's loving arms around her. She stood crying in the middle of a country road with her head just above the floodwater. And she didn't know how to swim! My gosh, sitting in a bathtub was scary and creepy.

The angry swirling wind knocked Zoey's balloon senseless, leaving it as helpless as a punching bag. "I can't steer it anymore," a beaten Hoover cried.

"Don't give up!" Zoey boomed.

Clunky called out, "This rain is so blinding. I can't even see Zoey's big belly. We'll never find Sally."

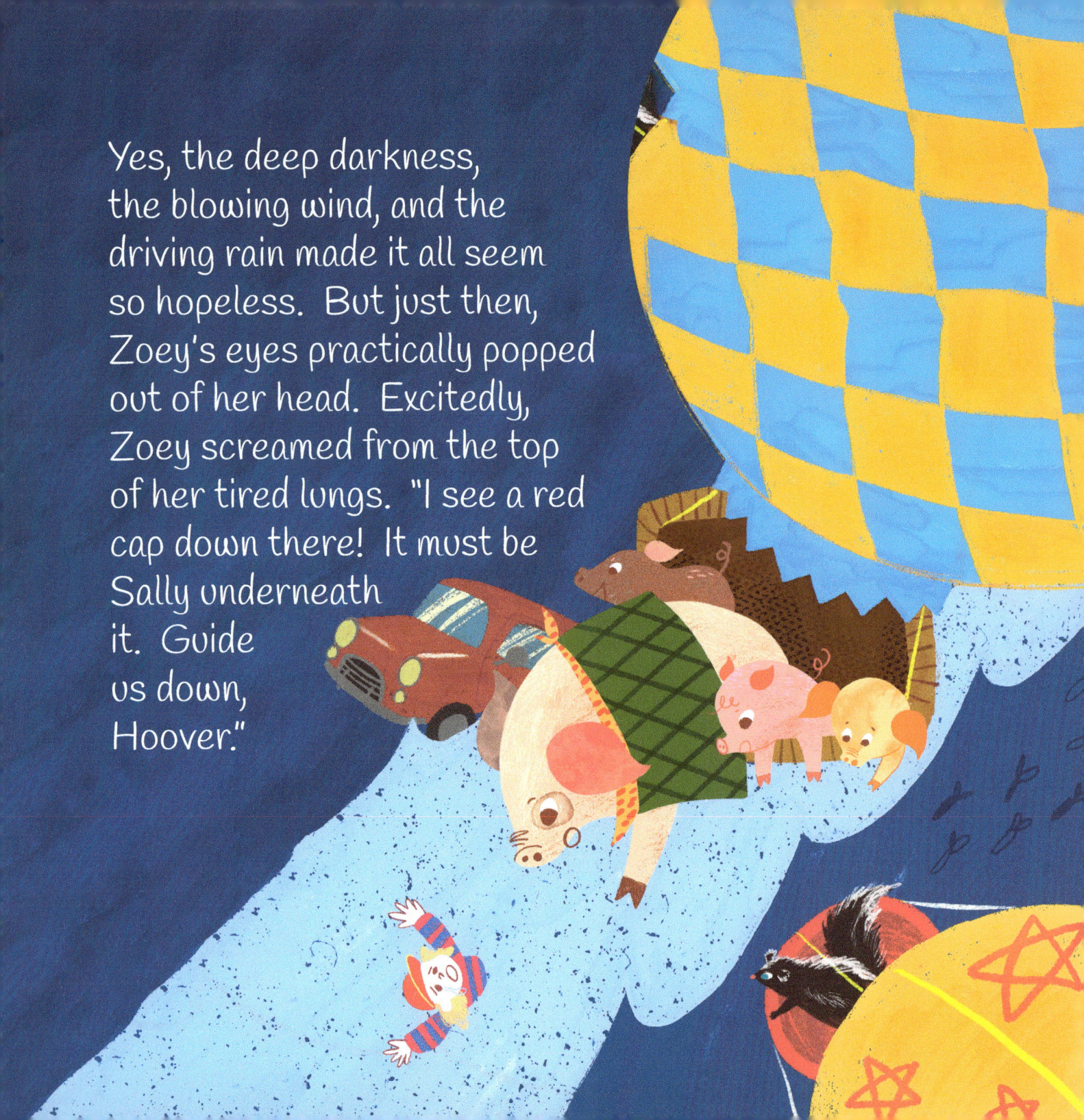

Yes, the deep darkness, the blowing wind, and the driving rain made it all seem so hopeless. But just then, Zoey's eyes practically popped out of her head. Excitedly, Zoey screamed from the top of her tired lungs. "I see a red cap down there! It must be Sally underneath it. Guide us down, Hoover."

But there was no way in a stinky man's happiest sour-milk dreams that Grandma Skunk and her gang were going to let Zoey get to Sally first. So the nasty skunks attacked Zoey's balloon with one-hundred-year-old stink bombs they had saved for special occasions. Poof!! Puff!! Poof!! the stink bombs sounded as they landed. Zoey, Hoover, Clunky, and Gloober battled back with slimy mud pies. Splat!! Splunk!! Kaboom!! they crackled as they pounded Grandma Skunk's balloon.

Sally cried, "Help me! Help me! I'm drowning!"

Zoey knew there wasn't any time to waste if Sally were to be saved. If the fight with Grandma Skunk continued to rage, all hope would be lost. So Zoey unselfishly shouted, "You win, Grandma Skunk. we give up. Just go rescue Sally."

Grandma Skunk yelled back, "Gladly, you fathead!"

But just then, a sudden gust of wind, more powerful than even Grandma Skunk's morning breath blew the skunk's balloon miles away. Zoey shouted, "Friends, take our balloon down. No time to lose."

Sally bravely struggled to lift her hands above the water as Zoey reached down and with all of her might plucked Sally up into the balloon.

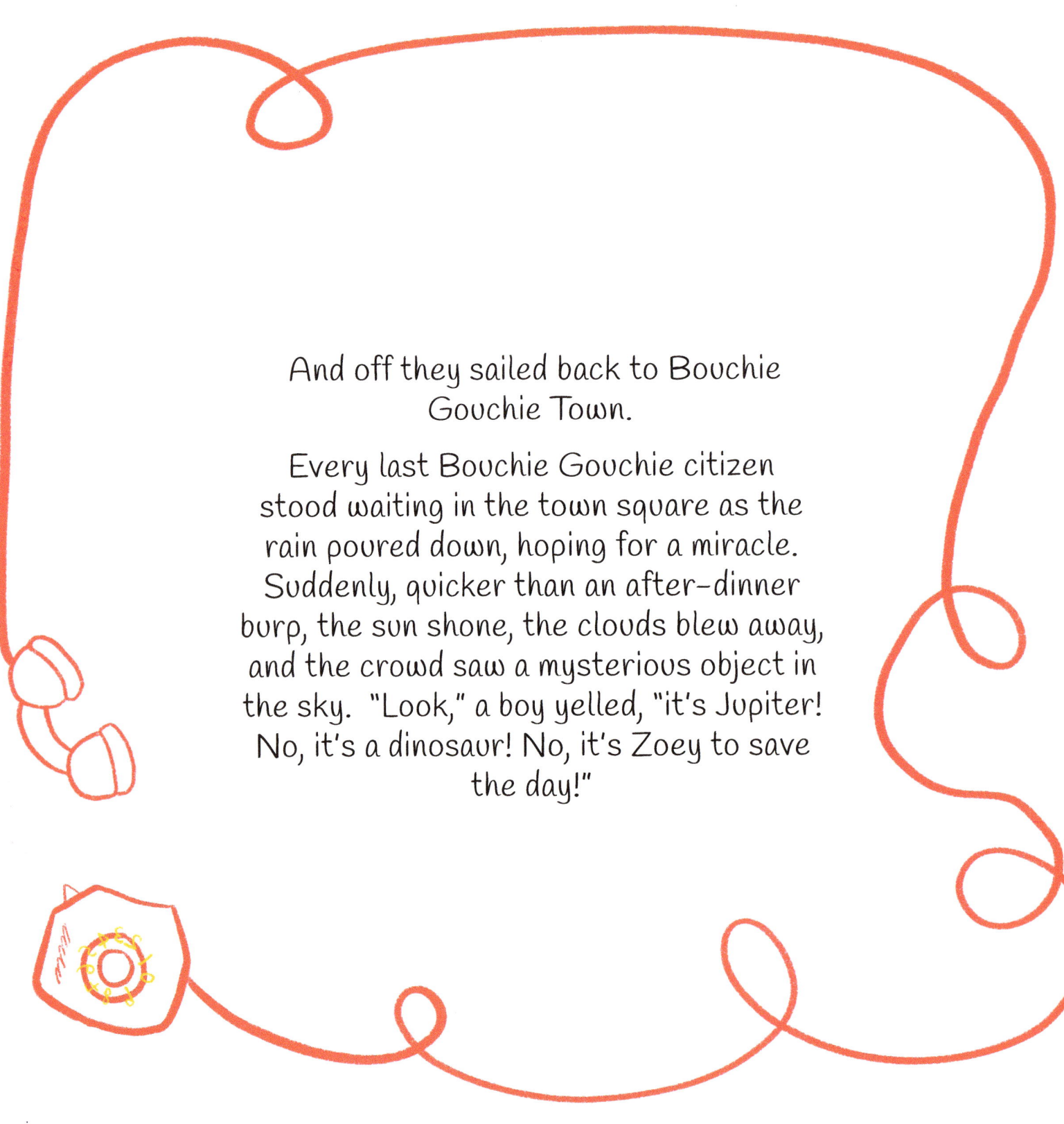

And off they sailed back to Bouchie Gouchie Town.

Every last Bouchie Gouchie citizen stood waiting in the town square as the rain poured down, hoping for a miracle. Suddenly, quicker than an after-dinner burp, the sun shone, the clouds blew away, and the crowd saw a mysterious object in the sky. "Look," a boy yelled, "it's Jupiter! No, it's a dinosaur! No, it's Zoey to save the day!"

Well, as the balloon touched down, everyone surrounded Zoey, Gloober, Clunky, Hoover, and Sally. Hugs and kisses were freely given to all. Sally's dad smiled and said, "Zoey, you're a heroine!"

Zoey looked down modestly and said, "No, it's my fault that all this happened in the first place. I just did what I had to do with a lot of help from my friends."

Farmer Gruder asked, "Zoey, did you learn anything?"

"You're darn right I did," Zoey bursting with joy, answered. "The easy way ends up being the hard way. Hey, everyone, come on over to my place.

I'll give you an egg. Real eggs. Ones that I gathered from Farmer Gruder's hens myself!"

I GIVE YOU AN EGG!

For these and other great books for children and young adults visit HistriaBooks.com